Little Book of Spine-Chilling Parlour Games

I0545246

Spine-chilling Parlour Games

The Mirror Game

What players needed:

- Mirror
- Candle

The Mirror Game

One popular game for young Victorian women was gathering in the dark and performing a ritual where each took a turn walking a flight of steps backward, holding a candle in one hand and a mirror in the other. As each progressed upward, she stared into the mirror, and if a man's face appeared, it would be that of the husband she would marry. But if the skull of the grim reaper appeared, she would die before she wed.

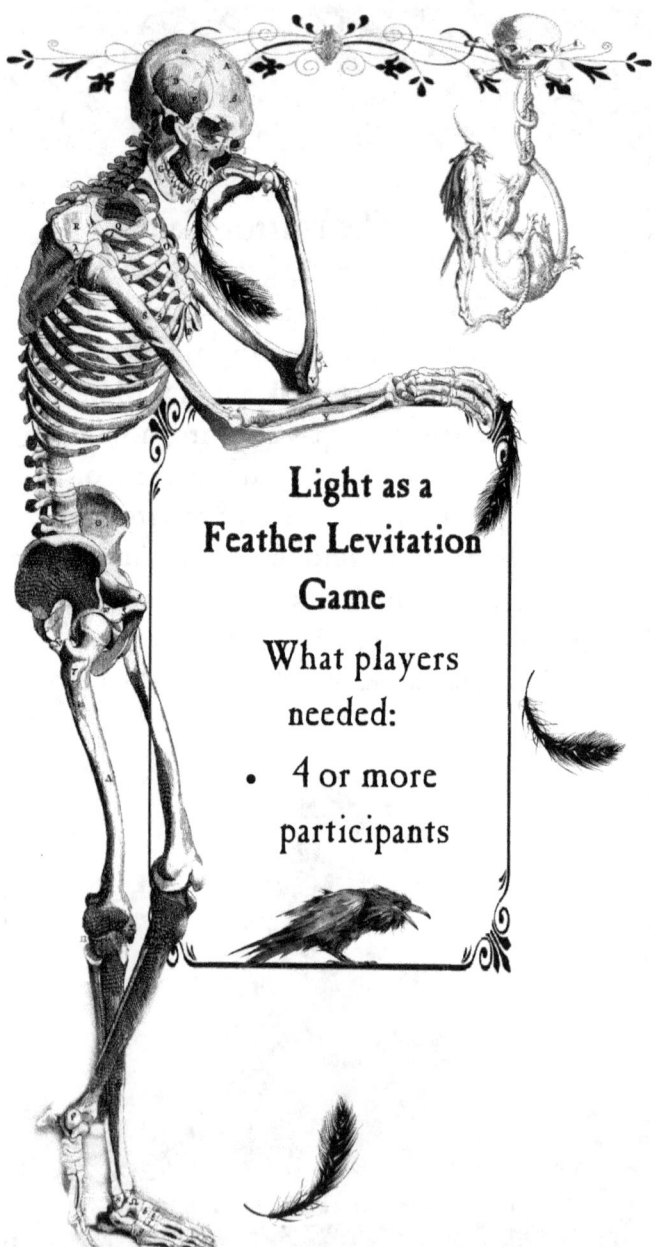

Light as a Feather Levitation Game

What players needed:

- 4 or more participants

 ## Light as a Feather Levitation Game

One person lies on their back flat on the floor. The rest space themselves around the person who is lying, stooping with one knee to the floor. The person at the head whispers into the ear of the person to the right, "I think she (or he) is sick." That person who received the words then whispers it to the person to their right, and so it is passed around to the third and fourth and until it makes it all the way back to the person at the head. This is done a second time with the words, "I believe she is getting sicker." All slip two fingers beneath the one lying flat. Next, the person at the head says, "I think she is dying," which is passed along, and then finally, "I think she is dead." Then all begin to chant, "Light as a feather, stiff as a board," while they lift (nearly effortlessly) the person off the ground.

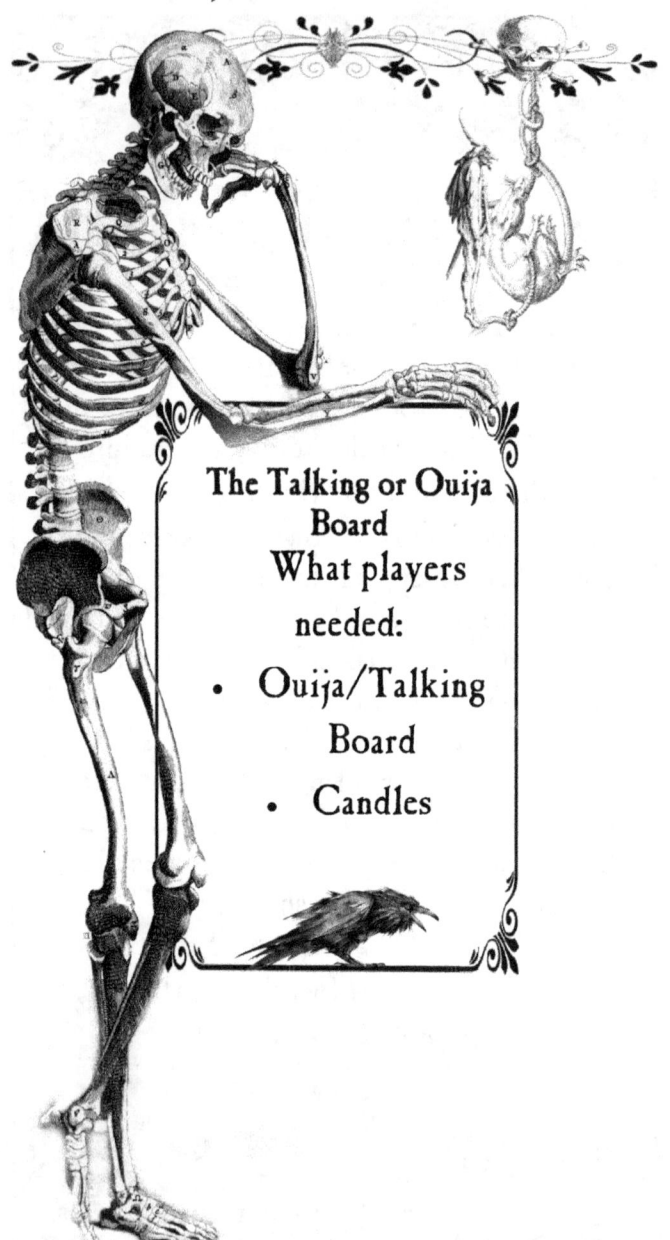

The Talking or Ouija Board
What players needed:

- Ouija/Talking Board
- Candles

The Talking or Ouija Board

The Talking Board or Ouija Board is used during a séance to communicate with the dead. It has letters and numbers, "yes" and "no" and "Goodbye" written on the board. Players place their fingers lightly on a small, heart-shaped planchette (or a glass cup) that moves via a spirit that spells out words to answer questions the players ask. The players light candles, darken the room, and then sit around the board. Each places two fingers on the planchette and takes turns asking questions from the spirit. The first question is usually, "Is there anyone here with us tonight?" Sometimes it may take a while for a spirit to arrive. Should a player feel a malevolent entity is communicating, they tell the spirit to go away, move the planchette to Goodbye, and flip the planchette over. Players should *never* forget to say "Goodbye," and remove fingers from the planchette and board when the game is concluded.

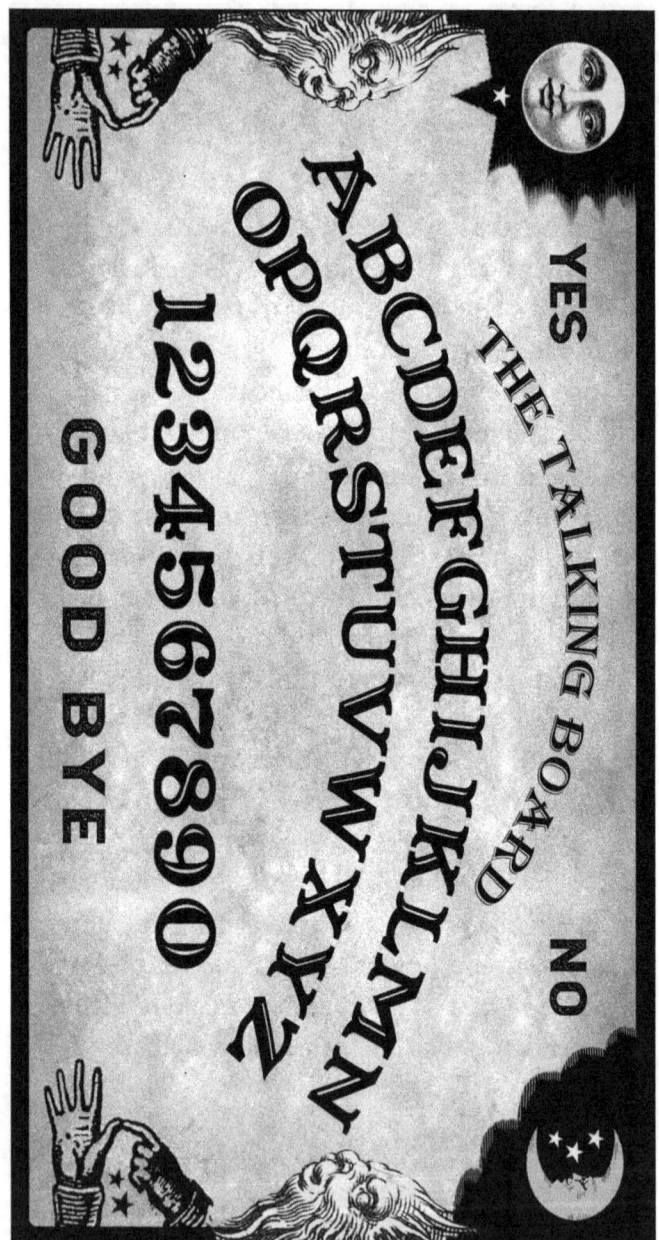

Questions to ask:

Are you here?

What is your name?

How many ghosts are here?

When did you die?

How did you die?

How many people are in this room?

How long ago did you die?

Do not forget to say Goodbye!

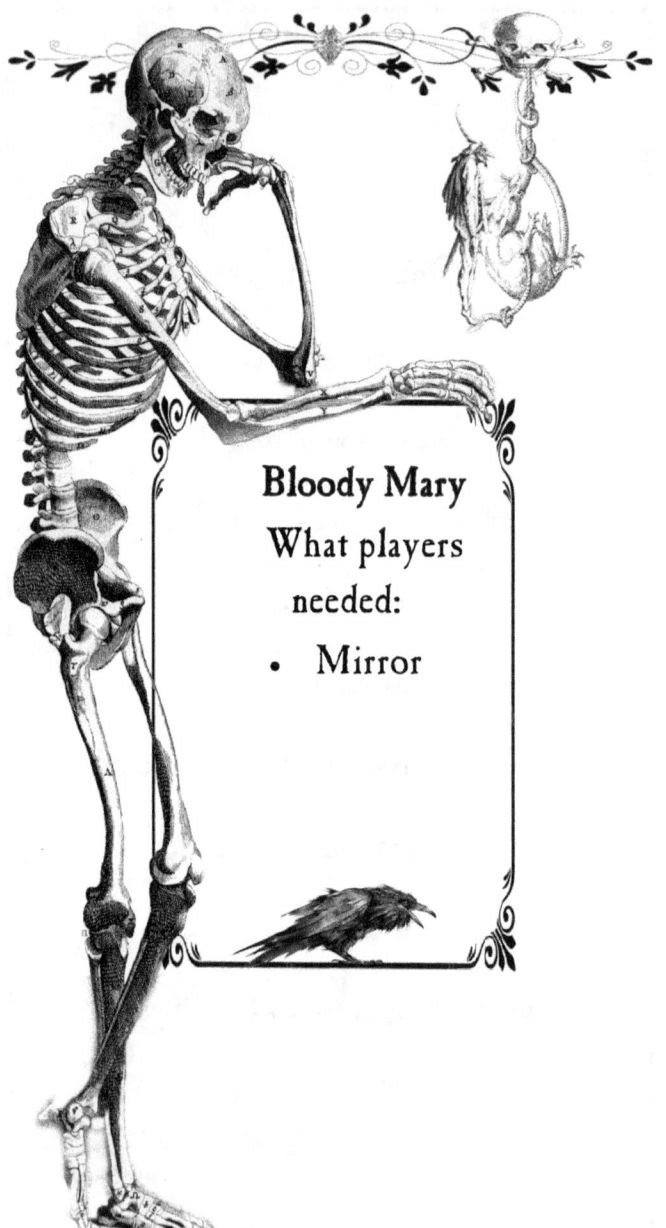

Bloody Mary

What players needed:

- Mirror

Bloody Mary

A player stands in front of a mirror in a dimly lit bathroom with the door shut and chants with eyes closed, "I believe in Bloody Mary" thirteen times. Then they open their eyes and stare into the mirror, waiting for a witch to appear covered in blood, screaming curses through the glass reflection.

The identity of Bloody Mary is believed to come from the 5-year reign in the 1500s of fervently Catholic Mary I. She seized the English throne and burned 280 Protestants at the stake as heretics. As a result, she was nicknamed Bloody Mary.

Bloody Mary

The Sandman

What players needed:

- Dark Room

The Sandman

The game requires two characters—the Storyteller and the Sleeper. Lights are dimmed. The Sleeper lies flat on the floor, face up and arms at sides. The Storyteller kneels beside the Sleeper and begins to gently touch the Sleeper while they tell a gruesome story of how the Sleeper died a horrible death. The Storyteller can use their hands to softly chop and hack off limbs, and at the end of the story, they pretend to fill the Sleeper up with sand. After the ritual, the Sleeper is asked to rise and feels as if their body is heavy and filled with sand.

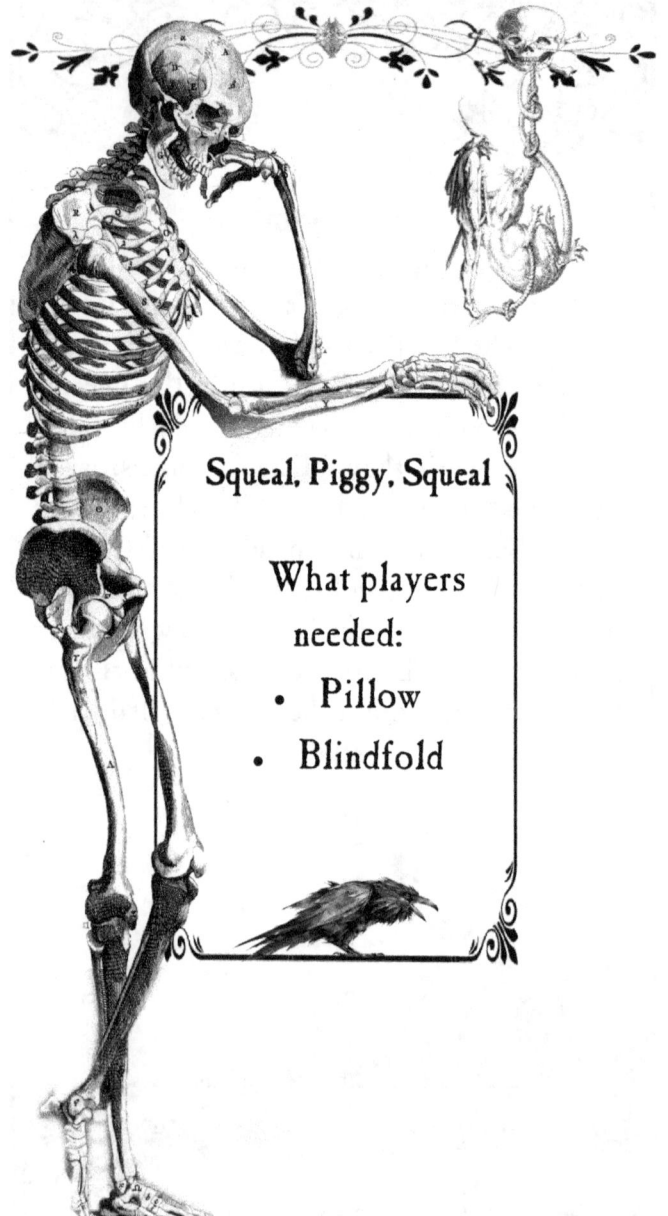

Squeal, Piggy, Squeal

What players
needed:

- Pillow
- Blindfold

Squeal, Piggy, Squeal

One player is a farmer, while the rest are piggies. The farmer holds a pillow in their grasp in the middle of the room, and someone places a blindfold on them. The piggies then move around the room before finding a place to sit while the farmer spins in a circle six times. The farmer then walks blindly around the room until he finds one sitting piggy. The farmer places the pillow on the piggy's lap, sits on top, and tells it to make a squealing sound. Then he must guess the name of the piggy. If he is correct, he becomes a piggy, and the piggy is the farmer. If not, he or she spins again and tries to locate another piggy.

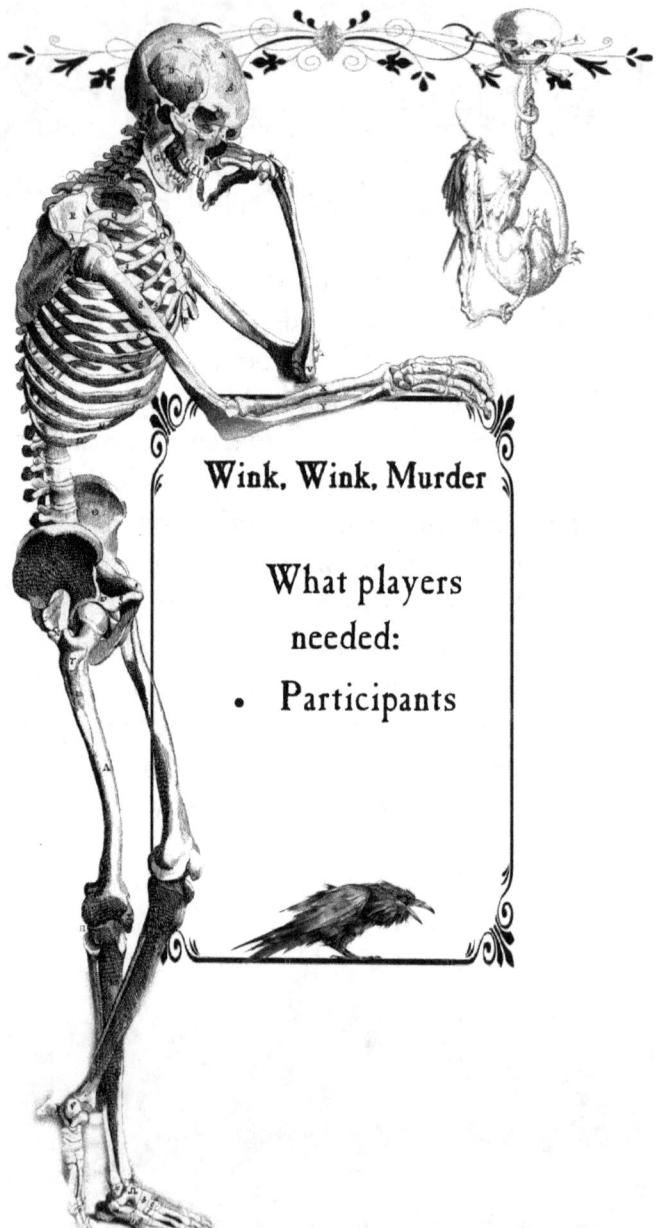

Wink, Wink, Murder

What players needed:

- Participants

Wink, Wink, Murder

One player is chosen as a detective who leaves the room long enough that a murderer can be secretly chosen amongst the players remaining. Those players then form a circle, and the detective returns and stands in the middle. The murderer secretly winks at players in the ring who immediately fall to the floor dead. The detective must guess who the murderer is from the remainder of the players standing in the circle.

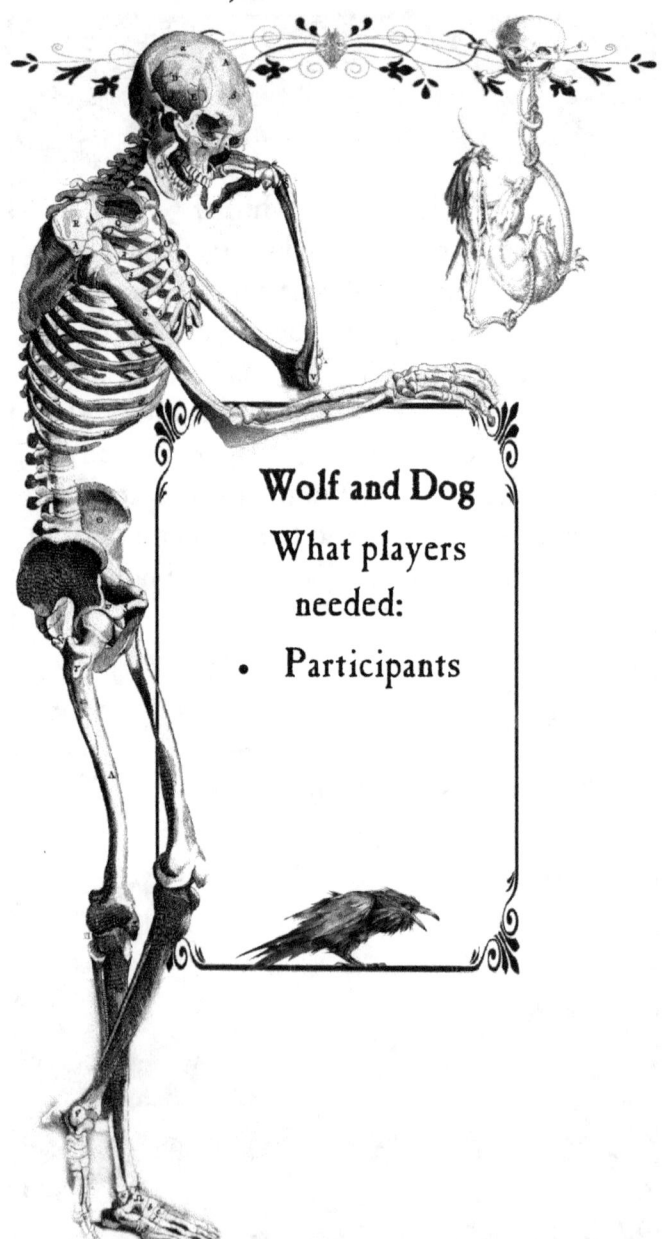

Wolf and Dog

What players
needed:

- Participants

Wolf and Dog

One person is the wolf. Another is the dog. Everyone else is the dog's tail and lines up behind the dog, holding on with one hand to the person's shoulder in front of them.

The wolf says, "I am a wolf, and I am going to eat you."

The dog says, "I am the dog, and no, you will not!"

Then the wolf says, "But I will at least taste a bit of your tail!"

So, the dog begins to run, dragging his people-tail along, while the wolf starts to chase the dog and tries to catch the last person of the tail.

If the wolf gets close, the dog can stop and defend the tail. If he does so, then the last person of the tail comes up in front of the dog and becomes the dog. If the first dog makes it to the back of the line before the wolf catches the tail, he wins.

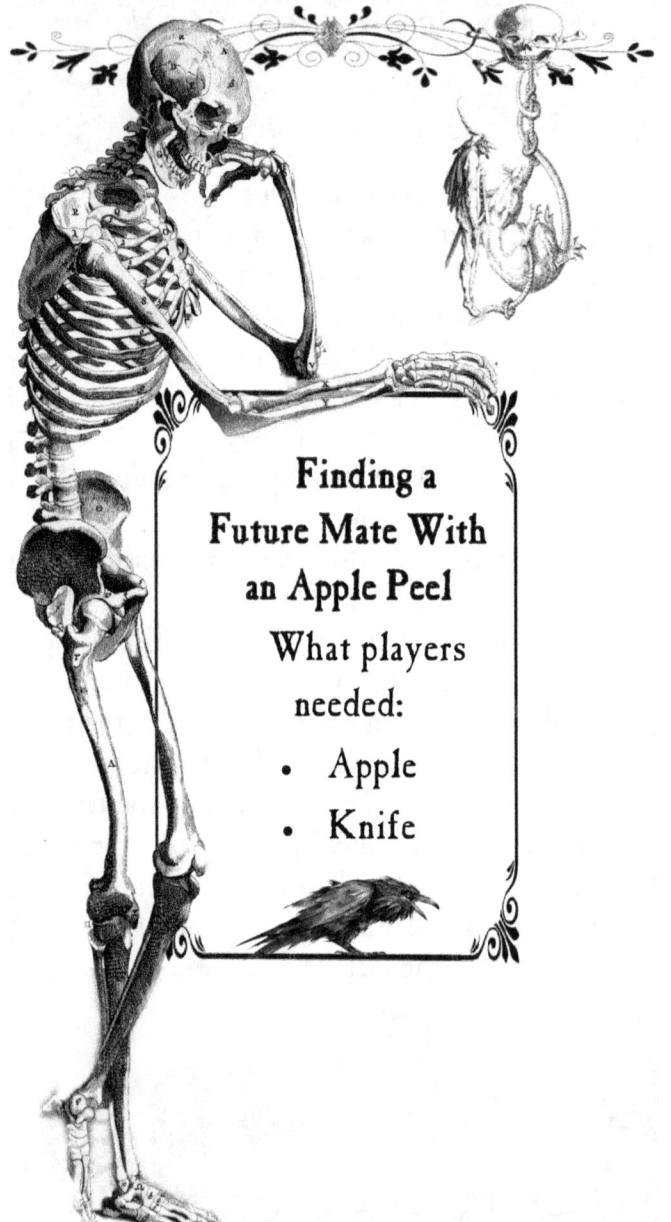

Finding a Future Mate With an Apple Peel

What players needed:

- Apple
- Knife

Finding a Future Mate With an Apple Peel

On the eve of Halloween, unmarried men and women would take an apple and pare the skin with a knife for as long as they could without stopping to get a lengthy spiral peel. They held a mirror in their right hand, staring into it while tossing the spiral over their left shoulder and onto the floor. Then they turned and looked at the apple peel spiral. Its shape would be the first letter of their future mate.

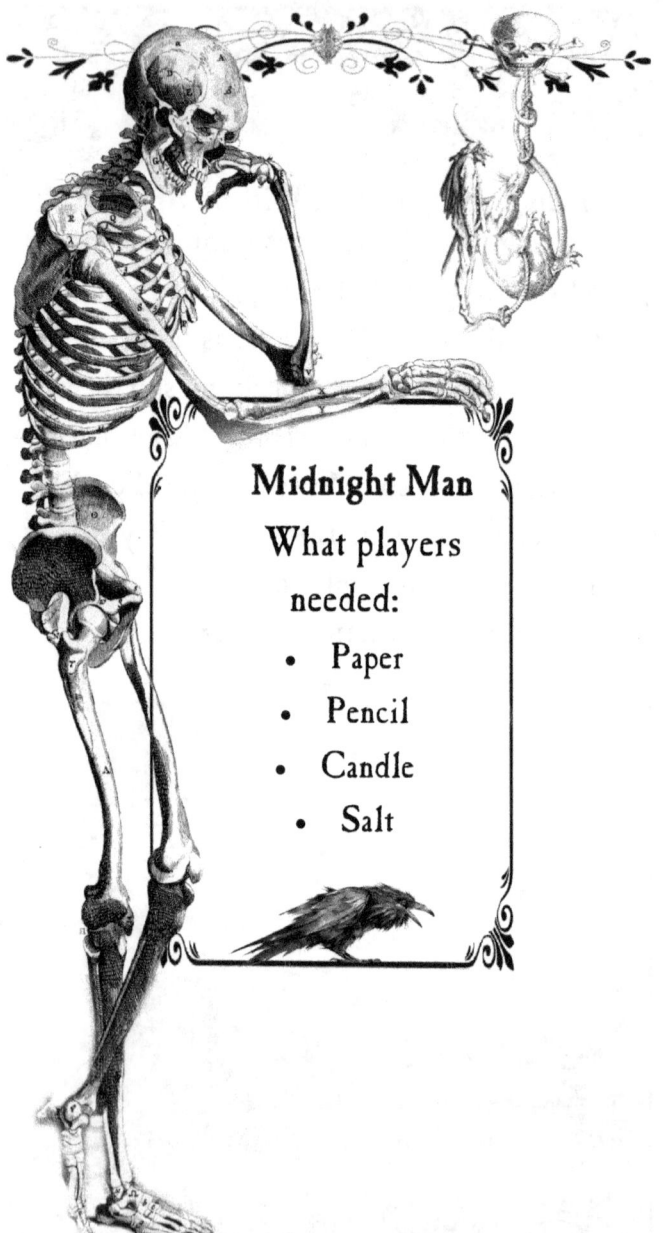

Midnight Man

What players needed:

- Paper
- Pencil
- Candle
- Salt

The Midnight Man

Each player writes their full name on a piece of paper and sets it on the floor in front of an entry door. On top of the papers, a candle is placed in a well-balanced holder and lit. Then one player knocks on the door 22 times, with the last knock precisely at midnight. Another player opens the front door, blows the candle out, then returns and closes the door. Once the door is shut, the candle is quickly relit. The Midnight Man, a mysterious, shadowy entity, is now in the home, and no one can leave. Until 3:33 a.m., everyone must keep moving inside to avoid the Midnight Man. Salt must be available—it is the only hope if the candle goes out as each of those within the home must make a circle with the salt around themself for protection until 3:33 a.m.

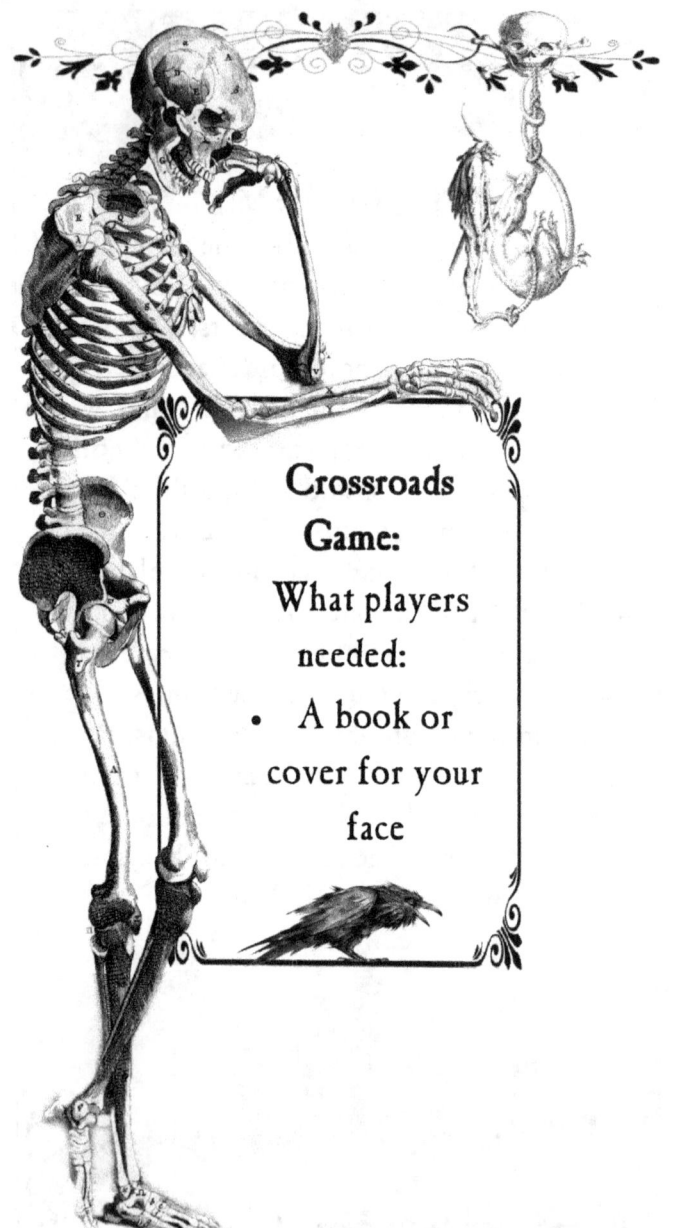

Crossroads Game:

What players needed:

- A book or cover for your face

Crossroads Game
(Tsuji-Ura)

The player walks out to a crossroads just after dark. They make a comb speak by rubbing fingers across the teeth three times. They say, "Tsuji-ura, tsuji-ura, grant me a true response." Now, the player waits for someone to pass. If it is a friend, the answer has been denied. If it is a stranger, the player covers their face and asks the stranger to tell their fortune. If there is no answer, the player must wait for another stranger. The game may be ended by leaving the crossroads.

This Japanese fortune-telling game came from early folklore and when crossroads were not filled with speeding cars. So, players must choose roads that are closed off from traffic, stand to the side, and bring a bystander for safety.

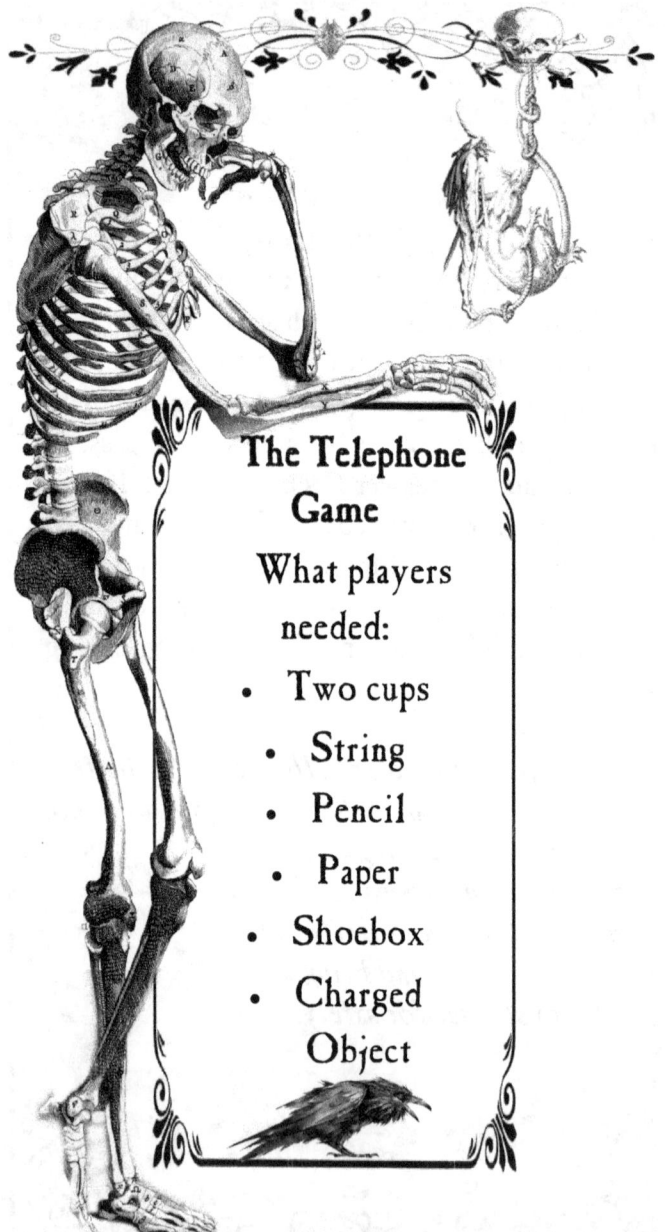

The Telephone Game

What players needed:

- Two cups
- String
- Pencil
- Paper
- Shoebox
- Charged Object

The Telephone Game

The player builds a cup phone by using the tip of a
pencil and poking one tiny hole in the bottom of two
plastic cups. Attach the cups by threading one end of
the string to each and knot to secure.

The player writes a letter to a dead person they wish to
contact, asking a question. This letter is read into one
cup. The player finds a charged object like a picture of
the person or item they owned. The charged item, the
cup not spoken into, and the letter are placed inside a
shoebox. The shoebox is closed, and the cup that was
spoken into is placed atop the shoebox. The shoebox is
left in a dark closest.

The player goes to bed to sleep. During the night, the
phone rings in the form of a dream, and when
awakened, the player goes to the closet and opens the
door. If the shoebox is open or the cup on top is
knocked off, the game ends, and the player must pull
the string from the phone. If not, the player enters the
closet and closes the door. They pick up the phone on
top of the box, place it against an ear, and listen. The
dead person will answer the question. Once finished,
the thread is tugged from the cup. The box is left in
the closet for three months.

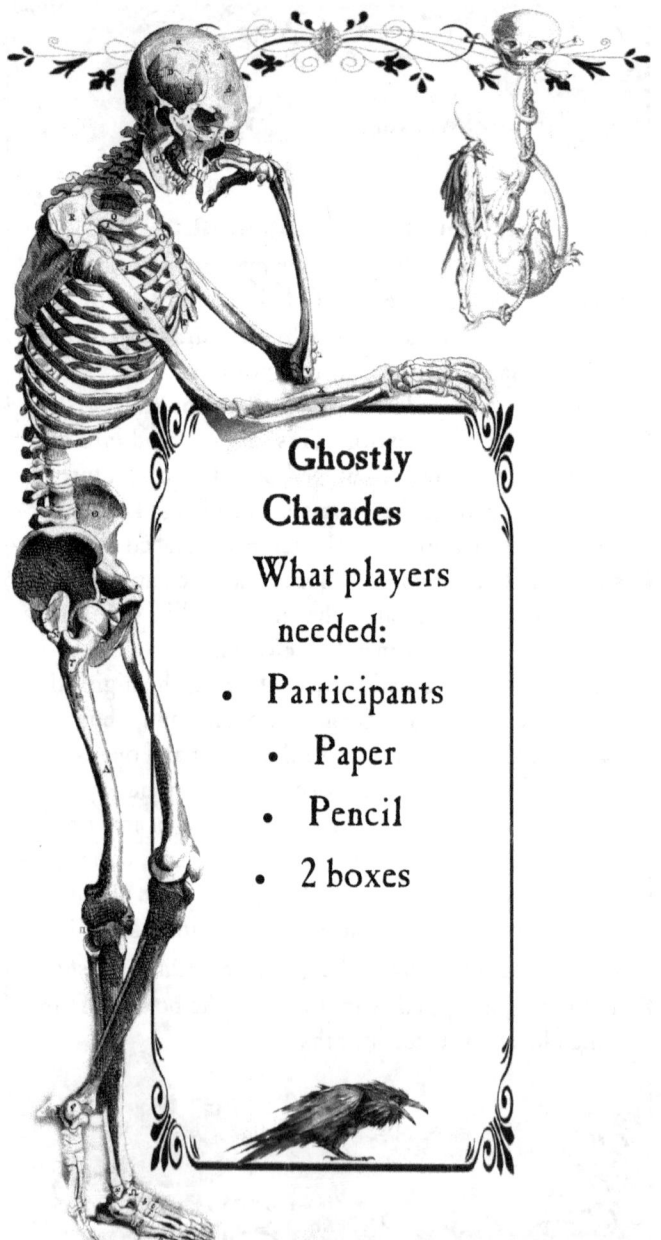

Ghostly Charades

What players needed:

- Participants
  - Paper
  - Pencil
  - 2 boxes

Charades with a Ghostly Twist

With the game of Charades, the objective is one team guessing a pantomimed phrase chosen by a competing team but acted out by their own team member.

Participants are divided into two groups. With the ghastly and ghostly in mind, each team writes down five themed words or phrases like a scary movie, book, or character in secrecy, each on a separate piece of paper. These pieces of paper are then folded several times and placed into a box. The boxes are exchanged, and one team member is selected to reach into the box and choose one of the pieces of paper. Without speaking to their teammates, they must act out what is on the sheet, and their teammates must guess what is written on the paper in an allotted amount of time.

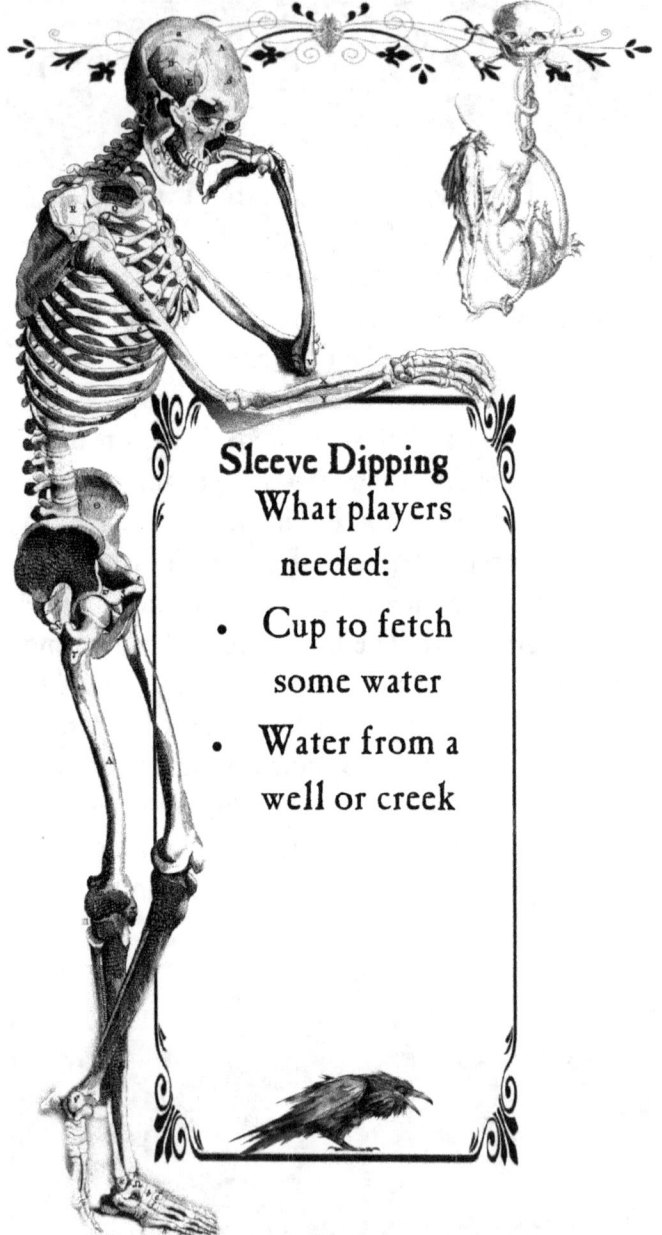

Sleeve Dipping
What players needed:

- Cup to fetch some water
- Water from a well or creek

Sleeve Dipping

Water is fetched from a well or creek where brides and burials pass over. Before going to bed, a sleeve is dipped into the water and the shirt hung up to dry at night. During the night, the future husband or wife will appear to turn the shirt over to dry on the other side.

Tell a Ghost Story

What players needed:

- A ghost story

Tell a Ghost Story
Like the Singing Bones, a Folktale of
Louisiana . . .

A large family with 25 children lived in a bayou below
New Orleans and all within one small, palmetto-roofed
shack. Food was scarce, and the mother had to divide
even the tiniest bit of fish or meat between all of them.

Many nights, the little ones would go to bed crying
because their bellies growled with hunger. It made the
wife always sullen and angry. She yelled at her husband
for this and that and even the smallest infraction like
smoking his pipe.

One winter was particularly hard, and the father came
home one night without any food for the children. He
stood outside the rickety house and pondered how he
would explain to his wife and children that he had no
food for them. Tears welled in his eyes as he imagined
the sad faces that would look up at him. Still, he took
the hard steps to the door and readied his hand to push
it open.

Yet, just as he entered, a wonderful scent of cooking meat tantalized his nostrils, and his happy children surrounded him. One snatched up his hand and pulled him inside, and his usually ill-tempered wife was smiling as she threw out her hand to expose the eating table. There was a feast of boneless meat sitting in front of him piled high in the center.

That night, the family enjoyed the finest meal they had eaten in years. But it would not be the last. For the next three days, the family indulged themselves in the delicious meat. The man thought about asking his wife where she got the meal, then decided it was not worth getting yelled at or putting her in a bad mood.

He also noticed that his wife was not eating with them, and he worried she was ill. So, he decided to use that notion to end his curiosity as he sat down for another supper. "This meat is delicious," the man said as he took a bite of a particularly tender, juicy piece. "But it must be expensive as it has no bones." She replied that she bought it that way, and without the bones, it was less weight to carry.

"Ah, I see. How about you sit and eat with us tonight?" the husband asked the wife. "I haven't seen you eat in days."

"I eat before you come home," she replied, "so I can care for the children."

He felt satisfied with her answer, but as he looked around the table, one of his favorite sons was missing.

He did not want to enrage his wife, so he did not mention anything aloud. But two weeks passed, and two more of their children did not greet him when he came home. He asked his wife where the children were, and she shrugged her shoulders, "I took them to their aunties house to visit," she answered. "They will be back in a while."

But they did not return. Another week passed, and still, another child disappeared. The man went for a walk and then returned, wondering how he would approach his wife. Something was wrong. He sat down hard on the back porch step, lit his pipe, and thought for a while. As he sat there, he heard a low humming nearby. At first, he thought it was a bird, then mosquitos. Yet it got louder the longer he listened. It was the sound of children singing, and it was coming from a rock near his foot. "Our mother kills us. Our father eats us. We have no coffins. We are not on holy ground—"
The man dropped to his knees and towed up the stone. Beneath it, he could see so many small children's bones! He gasped. Now he certainly knew where his children had gone. He knew where his wife had gotten the tender meat. He went inside the house, took up an axe, and killed the woman. He would not listen to her protests that there were too many children anyway. Then he buried the children in a cemetery, and he never ate meat again.

After telling the story, those hearing the ghostly tale take a walk past a cemetery. They listen carefully for the singing of the bones of the dead. But they must pass quickly and hold their breath lest they breathe in the spirit of someone who recently died.

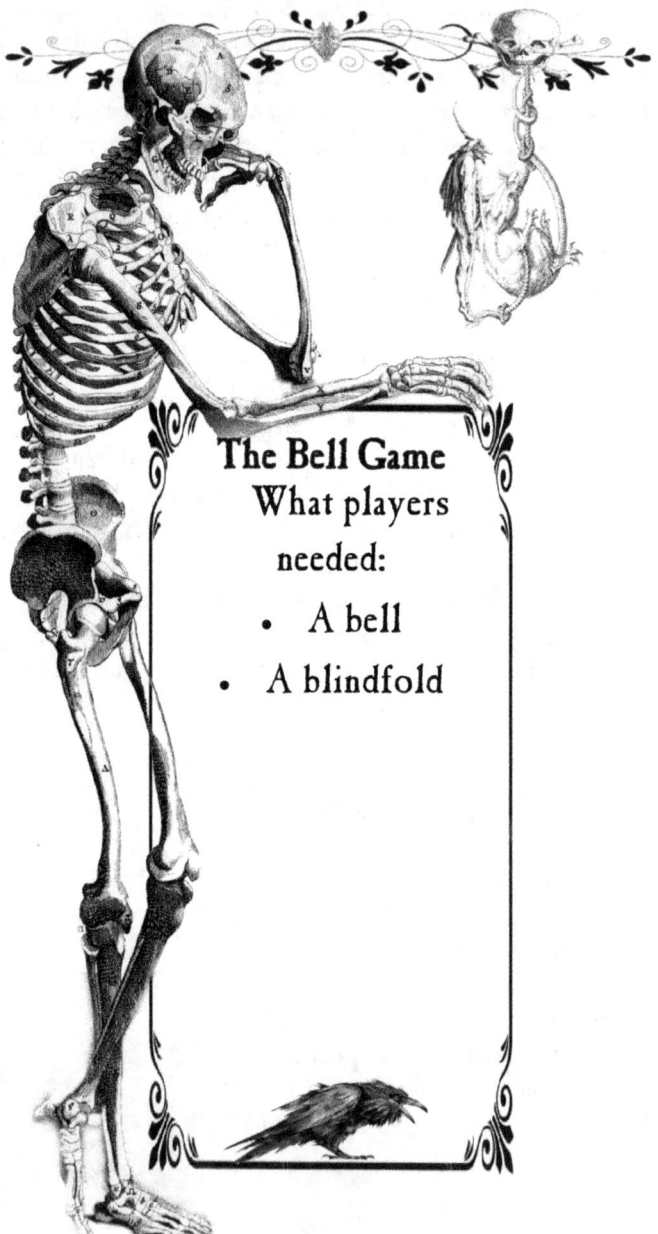

The Bell Game
What players
needed:

- A bell
- A blindfold

The Bell Game

It has long been believed that the ringing of bells repels evil spirits. In Rome, herders placed bells around lambs' necks to keep away wicked and wild beasts. Churches rang bells before a storm so the devils causing the squall might flee in fear that the sound of bells were messengers heralding the arrival of God. Bells were rung before bedtime to dispel the nighttime shades of death.

Bell games reflected those beliefs. One game, in particular, had all players blindfolded except for one they called the Bellman. The Bellman carried a small bell and strolled around a room while the blindfolded players (the ghosts) attempted to catch him or her. When someone caught the Bellman, the two exchanged places.

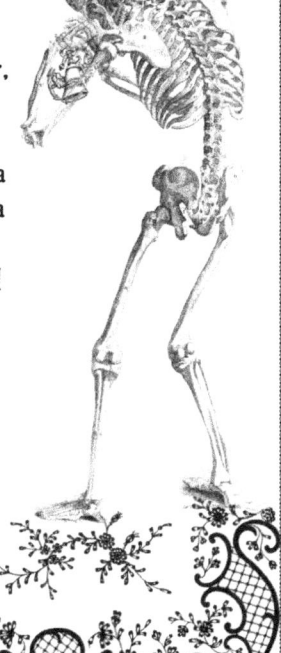

Citations—

Book of Parlour Games. (1854). The book of parlour games: Comprising explanations of the most approved games for the social circle, viz. Games of motion, attention, memory, mystification and fun, gallantry and wit, with forfeits, Penalties,

Fortier, A. (1895). Louisiana folk-tales: In French dialect and English translation.

Historical Halloween divination games and spells. Retrieved from https://www.interrobangtarot.com/blog/historical-halloween-divination-games-and-spells

Mangahasu.se. . Lovesick dead Retrieved from https://mangahasu.se/lovesick-dead/complete-c373450.html

Midnight Man Ritual. 2018, January 25. Midnight Man. Retrieved from https://sites.psu.edu/silenceofthenight/2018/01/25/midnight-man/

Scary games: 30 so spine-tingling they're addictive. 2019, May 20. Retrieved from https://bestlifeonline.com/scary-games/

Tsuji-URA, or the fortune game: How to play it. 2021, September 8. Retrieved from https://theghostinmymachine.com/2018/01/24/dangerous-games-tsuji-ura-fortune-game-crossroads-divination/

Devils—Afraid of bells. Retrieved from www.encyclopedia.com/science/encyclopedias-almanacs-transcripts-and-maps/devils-afraid-bells

Images: Public Domain/Purchase from the FG Waller Fund/Vilhelm Pedersen representation for the fairy tale "Ole Lukøje" by Hans Christian Andersen